"While we try to teach our children all about life,

our children teach us what life is all about."

Angela Schwindt

Good Night Little Lion Leo; Katharina Renteria

Copyright © 2014 by Katharina Renteria

Very special thanks to my good friend Deborah Paterson.

ISBN-10: 1512121215
ISBN-13: 978-1512121216

Good Night Little Lion Leo

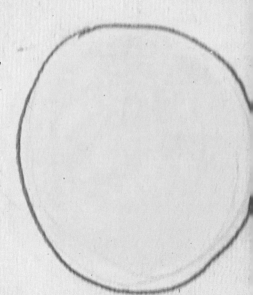

Written and illustrated
by Katharina Renteria

It is late at night,
the moon and stars are shining bright.
Happily, little cats are purring in their dreams.
All over the world it is bedtime so it seems.

High up in the mountains as you can see,
is living a very tired bear family.
They are all sleeping side by side,
cuddling each other through the night.

Even in the dessert in a faraway land
are camels resting in the sand.
All of them have already closed their big dark eyes,
if they hadn't they could see a thousand stars otherwise.

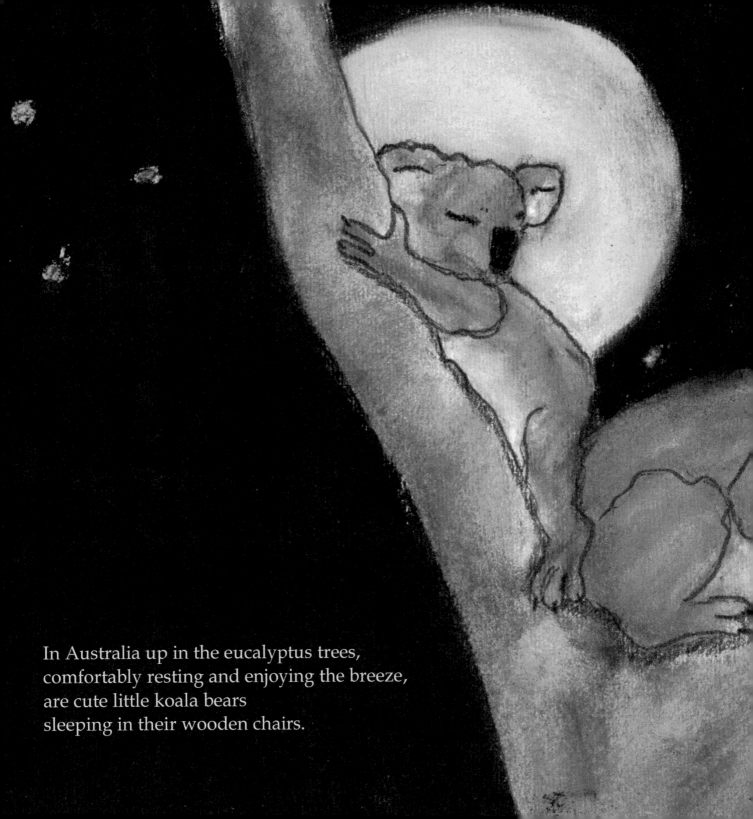

In Australia up in the eucalyptus trees,
comfortably resting and enjoying the breeze,
are cute little koala bears
sleeping in their wooden chairs.

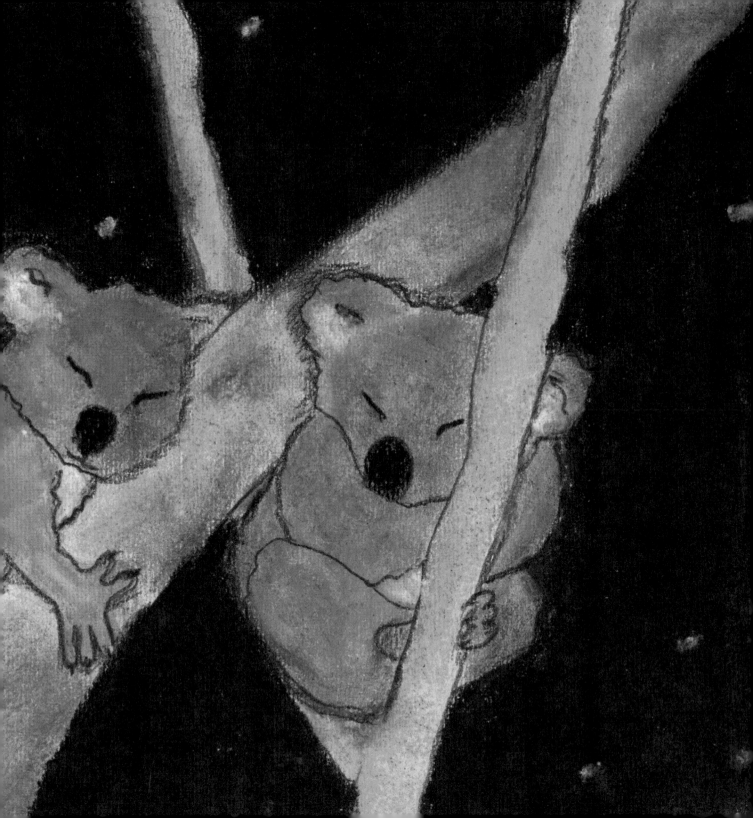

In Antarctica, surrounded by snow so white,
the sea lions are cuddling oh so tight.
All of them tired and sleepy,
now they're dreaming very deeply.

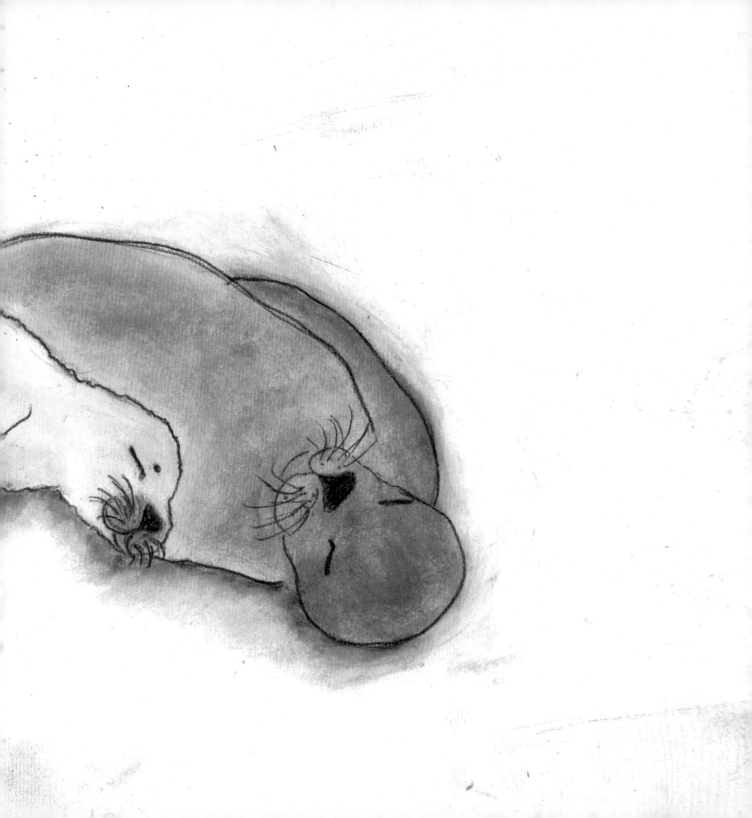

Deep inside the forest, in a hidden place,
wolves are sleeping face to face.
Hush hush, quiet is the night,
they will sleep until the return of light.

There is only one little boy still awake:
Can you hear the noise he makes?
It is a little lion called Leo
who is crawling up the tummy
of his very tired mummy.

His mother says,
shhh, my little boy, don't you see?
It is already bedtime for you and me!
Look at your daddy, can't you hear?
He is snoring and sleeping my sweet dear.

Leo whispers to his mother,
but mummy, look at the stars and the moon they are so nice!
I do not want to sleep and close my eyes!
All night long I am going to stay awake,
And I will enjoy it with every breath I take.

His mother smiles and looks above,
my little Leo, my dear love,
do you know how many stars there are?
Wouldn't it be nice to count each star?

So little Leo starts counting,
one, two, three and four … oh sigh,
five, six, seven, eight … oh my!
are there no more stars left in the sky?
Look, Leo can't keep his eyes open
and the last numbers are left unspoken.

Little Leo fell asleep softly together with his dad.
Mother Lion smiles and cuddles him in bed.
She gives him a little kiss, just a gentle touch,
and whispers, "I do love you" so very very much!

Good Night
Little Lion
Leo!

Coming soon by the end of 2015:

Big Brother, Little Sister
Big Brother, Little Brother
Big Sister, Little Sister
Big Sister, Little Brother

A story for children who are
expecting their little brother or sister.

74135509R00015

Made in the USA
San Bernardino, CA
13 April 2018